ANNABEL the ACTRESS

STARRING IN

Hound of the Barkervilles

ANNABEL the ACTRESS

STARRING IN

Hound of the Barkervilles

By **Ellen Conford**

Illustrated by **Renee W. Andriani**

SIMON & SCHUSTER BOOKS FOR YOUNG READERS
New York London Toronto Sydney Singapore

SIMON & SCHUSTER BOOKS FOR YOUNG READERS
An imprint of Simon & Schuster Children's Publishing Division
1230 Avenue of the Americas, New York, New York 10020

The text for this book is set in Berkeley.
Printed in the United States of America

2 4 6 8 10 9 7 5 3 1

Library of Congress Cataloging-in-Publication Data
Conford, Ellen.
Annabel the actress, starring in the hound of the Barkervilles / by
Ellen Conford ; illustrated by Renee W. Andriani.
p. cm.
Summary: When Annabel, who wants to be a famous actress
someday, has a part in a real play, she finds she must cope with a
big dog and an unruly audience member.
ISBN 0-689-84734-3
[1. Theater—Fiction. 2. Actors and actresses—Fiction. 3. Dogs—
Fiction. 4. Humorous stories.] I. Andriani, Renee, W.., ill. II. Title
PZ7.C7593 Anv 2002
[Fic]—dc21   2001042848

To Eileen Moushey, of Mysteries by Moushey,
with heartfelt thanks for her close friendship and
invaluable technical assistance

A Mysterious Phone Call

Annabel was an actress. She wasn't a famous actress yet. But she knew she would be someday. It was only a matter of time.

Meanwhile, she worked hard to prepare for her career. She read everything she could find about actors and acting. And she practiced every day.

Today she was practicing being mysterious.

She tiptoed around the dining room. She ducked beneath a chair. She pressed her fingers against her lips.

I have a deep, dark secret, she thought. *And no one must find me.*

She heard her father's steps on the basement stairs. She darted behind a window curtain.

"Heh heh heh," she chuckled softly. "Heh

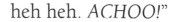

heh heh. *ACHOO!*"

"Annabel?" her father said. "Is that you back there?"

She stuck her head out between the curtains. "Yes," she said.

"What are you doing?" he asked.

"I'm sneaking and lurking," she said. "I have a mysterious secret."

She came out from behind the curtains. "Did I seem mysterious to you?"

"Not very," her father said.

"The curtains are dusty," Annabel said. "It's hard to be mysterious when you're sneezing."

Her father went into the kitchen. He came back carrying a flashlight and a large screwdriver.

"What are those for?" Annabel asked.

"The dryer is broken," her father answered.

"Do you know how to fix it?"

"A dryer is a very simple machine," her father said. "I probably just have to replace a fuse, or something."

"That's good." Annabel was already tiptoeing around the dining room again. *I have a deep, dark secret,* she told herself.

"Annabel?" She heard her father's voice from the stairs.

"Yessss?" She made her voice low and mysterious.

"Don't tiptoe down here and sneak up on me."

"I wouldn't do that!" Annabel said. But she wished she had thought of it.

The phone rang. Annabel ran to pick up the receiver. "Annabel the Actress," she announced. "No part too big or too small."

"Good!" a woman's voice said. "Just the person I wanted to speak to."

"Really?" Annabel tried not to sound too excited. But she hadn't had a good part in a long time.

"My name is Barbara Wells," the woman on the phone said. "I direct a theater group that presents mystery plays."

"I love mysteries!" Annabel said. "As a matter of fact, I was just practicing being mysterious."

"What a coincidence," Barbara said. "Have you ever done an interactive play?"

Annabel thought about it. She wasn't sure what *interactive* meant. But she had a feeling she hadn't done it.

"What we do," Barbara went on, "is perform a mystery play. And the audience has to solve the mystery."

"That sounds interesting," Annabel said.

"Oh, it is!" Barbara Wells said. "But besides being an actor, you have to be a quick thinker."

Annabel didn't know why she would have to be a quick thinker to be in the play. But she was pretty sure she was one.

"Carol Boxer said you were a good actress," Barbara went on. "I think you go to school with her son, Lowell?"

"Lowell?" Annabel repeated. "Lowell Boxer?"

Lowell Boxer was Annabel's lifelong enemy. He had teased her and picked on her since first grade. Making Annabel miserable made Lowell Boxer happy.

"Is Lowell going to be in the play, too?"

"Oh, no," Barbara Wells said. "There's only one child in the play. I'd like you to try out for the part."

"Oh!" cried Annabel. "Oh, yes!"

A real, live stage play . . . in a real theater! Until now, Annabel had only been in class plays at school.

"You have a nice, clear speaking voice," Barbara said. "And if you can think on your feet, you might be just right for the part."

"Thank you!" Annabel said.

"Just one more thing," Barbara said. "You're not afraid of dogs, are you?"

"Uh . . ."

Annabel wasn't exactly afraid of dogs. But she didn't exactly love them, either.

"Good!" said Barbara Wells. "Binky and I are both eager to meet you."

Scene 2

The Paw Prints of an Enormous Hound

Her mother waited in the car as Annabel walked up the driveway to Mrs. Wells's door.

A short woman wearing a long skirt and a purple sweater opened the door. "You must be Annabel," she said.

"Yes." Annabel was suddenly very nervous. She could see a group of people talking and laughing in the living room behind Mrs. Wells.

"And I'm Barbara," Mrs. Wells said. She waved at Annabel's mother. "I'll phone you when we're done," she called. "We won't be too late."

"Bye, Mom!" Annabel waved also. Her mother tooted the horn and drove away.

Annabel followed Barbara into the living room. The actors stopped chatting when they saw her. A dark woman with long, shiny hair raised her soda can.

"Hi," she said. "Don't be nervous. We don't bite."

Annabel tried not to think about Binky, the dog she wasn't supposed to be afraid of.

"I'm not nervous," she said nervously.

"Annabel is trying out for the role of Polly Morfus," Barbara said.

A tall man with a thin black mustache leaned over to shake Annabel's hand.

"Manning Marlowe," he introduced himself. He gave Annabel a little bow.

Annabel was surprised at the bow. She wasn't sure what she should do, so she bowed back.

"Manning plays Harley Golightly, the international sportsman and playboy," Barbara said. "And this is the rest of our cast."

"I'm Janice Taylor." The dark-haired woman smiled at Annabel again. "I play Senorita Lolita Lopez," she said. "I am mysterious and glamorous."

"Wow," said Annabel. "Just yesterday I was practicing being mysterious. But glamorous is probably a lot harder."

"Stan Taylor," Barbara went on. "He will be Axel Greece, the chauffeur. Betsy Cohen, who'll play Lady Ashley Grate. And Harvey Tuttle. He's your father, the butler."

"Pleased to meet you," Annabel said.

"And I play Mrs. Van Barkerville. Now, I know you want to see your part."

Your part! Barbara had said "your part" as if Annabel were already a member of the cast!

She handed Annabel a script with a light blue cover. It said, HOUND OF THE BARK-ERVILLES.

"I like the title," Annabel said.

"Thank you," said Barbara. "I wrote the play myself."

"Uh—speaking of dogs," Annabel said, "where's Binky?"

"He's in the bedroom," Barbara said. "I'll let him out to meet you later."

"No hurry," Annabel said.

"Let's start reading on page one," said Barbara. "Your lines are underlined in yellow."

"Okay." Annabel started reading to herself. She read all the lines marked in yellow. She looked through the script to see how many lines she had.

From somewhere in the house, she heard whining and thumping sounds. She tried to ignore them. It wasn't easy.

Polly's part wasn't very big. Annabel was sure she could memorize it in a day or two.

YOWWLLLL!

Annabel dropped her script.

"Binky hates to be left alone," Barbara said. "I'd better let him out of the bedroom before he breaks the door down."

Annabel gulped. She moved toward the couch, and stood next to Betsy Cohen.

"Don't be afraid of Binky," Betsy said. "He's really just a big pussycat."

"I'm not afraid," Annabel said. But her voice squeaked like Minnie Mouse.

WOOF!

Annabel heard paws pounding on the wooden floor.

"Binky, calm down!" Barbara ordered.

The biggest dog Annabel had ever seen galumphed into the living room.

Annabel couldn't move. Her eyes grew wide. She stared at Binky. Binky stared back at Annabel.

Then he bounded across the room and jumped.

"Yikes!" Annabel ducked under the coffee table. A huge black nose followed her under the table. It poked her in the ear. A giant tongue slurped across her cheek.

"ACK!" she yelled.

"He likes you," Barbara said.

Binky started licking Annabel's hair.

"Has he eaten today?" Annabel asked.

Barbara tugged at the dog's red collar. "Come, Binky!"

Binky backed out from under the table.

"Binky, sit!" Barbara commanded.

Binky sat. But he lowered his head and stared at Annabel. His tongue hung out of the side of his mouth.

"I thought you weren't afraid of dogs," Barbara said.

"Are you sure he's a dog?" Annabel asked.

"Binky's a Newfoundland," said Barbara. "They are a large breed."

"Large?" Annabel repeated weakly. Binky was almost as big as a Jeep. A dog named Binky ought to be small and cute. Like a beagle, or a toy poodle. Or one of those tiny dogs with long, silky hair and dainty paws.

Annabel tried to catch her breath. She thought of Winona McCall, her favorite actress.

Winona had had to work among lions and leopards and rhinoceroses while she was filming *Into Africa.*

I am calm, Annabel told herself. *I don't have to work with lions and rhinoceroses. I just have to work with a huge dog the size of a Jeep.*

I am calm, Annabel repeated to herself. She took a deep breath and crawled out from under the table. She stood up.

Binky stretched his head toward her and panted. A thin string of drool dangled from his tongue.

Stan Taylor patted Annabel on the shoulder.

"Hey, it's okay, kid," he said. "I did the same thing the first time I met Binky."

She Was Only the Butler's Daughter

"I think I got the part because I didn't have a heart attack when Binky jumped on me," Annabel said.

Annabel and her friend Maggie were in Annabel's room, looking at Annabel's script. Maggie was going to help Annabel practice her lines.

"You must have read your part very well," Maggie said.

"Barbara hardly had me read anything," Annabel said. "She didn't even ask me any practice questions."

"What are practice questions?" Maggie asked.

"After we do the play," Annabel explained, "the whole cast has to mingle with the audience. They ask us questions to try and figure out who kidnapped Binky."

"What's your costume going to be?" Maggie asked.

Maggie knew everything about fashion. She was a very stylish dresser. She was going to be Annabel's costume designer when Annabel was a star.

"I don't know," Annabel said. "I guess Barbara will give me a costume. Or I could wear my own clothes. I'm only the butler's daughter."

"Oh. Well, maybe next time you'll wear something glamorous," Maggie said.

Annabel's part, Polly Morfus, was very small. But it was mysterious, and there was a really dramatic moment when Polly came running into the party, crying that Binky was gone.

"My lines are underlined in yellow," Annabel told Maggie. "You read the last words just before them. Those are my cues."

Maggie looked at the script. "Wow, you're right on the first page," she said. She cleared her throat and began. "Hurry, Polly. It's early to bed for you tonight."

"Are there going to be a lot of people at the party tonight, Father?" Annabel recited.

"A lot of rich people," Maggie read. "Why, the jewels in this house tonight will be worth a king's ransom."

"I hope the Crestview jewel thief doesn't know about the party," Annabel said.

"Hey, you've already memorized your lines!" Maggie said.

"Well, there aren't very many of them," Annabel said.

"You're supposed to give the butler a meaningful look," Maggie read. "What does that mean?"

"It's a clue," Annabel told her. "Before my father became a butler, he was a jewel thief. When he got out of jail, he changed his name to Abel Morfus, and got this job as Mrs. Van Barkerville's butler."

"Cool!" said Maggie. "Is he the kidnapper?"

"No, just one of the suspects. I'm a suspect too," Annabel said.

"Cooler! Can I come and see the play?"

"It's grown-ups only," Annabel told her. "The play is to raise funds for the Friends of the Arts."

It didn't take much longer to rehearse Annabel's lines. There were only eight of them.

"You are definitely ready," Maggie said. "You know your part perfectly."

After Maggie went home, Annabel decided that she should practice answering some questions. Barbara might want to test her quick thinking at the first rehearsal.

Her mother was in the kitchen doing a crossword puzzle.

"I have to practice for the play," Annabel told her. "Could you ask me a question?"

Her mother looked up from the puzzle. "What's a four-letter word for coffee-cup holder?"

"I don't know," Annabel said. "But I don't think anybody at the play is going to ask me that."

"Probably not." Her mother frowned. "Let me think." She tapped her pencil against her nose. "Okay. Do you know who did it?"

"No," said Annabel.

"Well, when did—" Her mother stopped.

"I don't know what to ask," she said. "I haven't read the play yet."

Annabel sighed deeply.

She went downstairs to the basement. Maybe her father could think of some questions to ask her.

When she got to the laundry room, she saw her father's legs sticking out from behind the dryer. She heard screeching noises, like the scraping of metal. Then she heard a loud groan. Her father crawled out from behind the dryer.

"Did you fix it yet?" Annabel asked.

"Does it look like it's fixed?" he answered.

The drum that tumbled the clothes sat on top of the washing machine. Metal parts and tools were scattered all over the basement floor. The dryer door was leaning against the oil burner.

"Not really," Annabel said.

Her father picked up a bolt and some screws. He stared at them. He flicked his flashlight on, then turned it off. He put the screws down. He turned the flashlight on again and pointed the beam at Annabel.

"Did you want something?" he growled.

"Not really," she said.

Scene 4

Walking the Dog

On Wednesday night, Annabel's father drove her to Barbara's house for the first rehearsal of *Hound of the Barkervilles*.

The front door was open. Through the glass outer door, Annabel could see a huge black head. A huge black nose was pressed against the glass.

"Good grief!" her father said. "Is that Binky?"

"I told you he was big," Annabel said.

"You were right." Her father was in a much better mood now that he had fixed the dryer. "You're not afraid of him?"

"Winona McCall worked with lions and rhinoceroses in *Into Africa*," Annabel said. "And she won an Academy Award. So I guess I can work with the biggest dog I've ever seen in my entire life."

She got out of the car and walked up the driveway to the front steps. When Binky saw her, his whole body started to wriggle with excitement. She could see him drooling before she even reached the door.

She turned toward the car. "I'll call you when rehearsal's over," she told her father. "And could you bring me some dry clothes?"

Barbara held Binky's collar so Annabel could get inside. She had barely made it through the door when Binky started licking her. He licked her hand. He poked his nose in her neck. He wiped the side of his mouth on her arm.

"He's so happy to see you," Barbara said.

Annabel wiped her arm on her shirt. "He could be a little less happy," she said. "I wouldn't mind."

"Janice and Stan Taylor aren't here yet," Barbara told her. "I thought we could go over some questions that the guests might ask you."

"I think that would be a good idea," Annabel said. "I wanted to practice answering questions at home, but—"

Binky licked Annabel's ear. She shuddered, and rubbed her ear.

"Binky, sit!" Barbara commanded. Binky sat.

Annabel said hi to the other actors. Then she and Barbara sat down near the fireplace.

"When people ask you questions," Barbara began, "you can't lie. You have to answer truthfully."

Binky lay down. He started wiggling toward Annabel.

"But what if someone asks me who the kidnapper is?" Annabel said.

"You don't lie," Barbara said. "But if someone asks you a question you can't answer, create a diversion."

"What does that mean?" Annabel asked.

Binky crept along the floor on his belly, moving closer to Annabel. She watched him out of the corner of her eye as she tried to listen to Barbara.

"A diversion is when you distract someone," Barbara answered. "You can burst out crying, or get angry and throw a tantrum. Or you could get scared and run away. That way you avoid answering the question."

Binky had worked his way right up to Annabel's chair. He sat up, and put his huge head in her lap. She sat very still and tried to ignore him.

"I am very good at crying and screaming."

Drool from Binky's wet mouth began to soak through her jeans. Annabel felt her lap getting wetter and wetter. But she did not cry or scream.

When Janice and Stan arrived, Barbara began the rehearsal. Annabel had no trouble with her opening lines. Then she had to wait for a bit, till the scene where she took Binky to the chauffeur.

She was more worried about this part of the play than anything else. Yes, Binky knew the command "Sit!" even if he couldn't do it for very long. But did he know "Walk without knocking anybody over?"

At her cue, Annabel said, "All right, Father. I hope the party is a great success, Mrs. Van Barkerville."

She picked up Binky's leash and led him around the living room. In the real performance, she would have to lead him across the stage.

She walked him from the living room into

the dining room. He followed her perfectly, walking right next to her left leg, and not trying once to knock her over.

"That was excellent!" Annabel said, surprised. She patted Binky's head lightly. "Good dog." Binky thumped his tail so hard that teacups rattled in the china cabinet.

Annabel's next line was the most dramatic moment in the play. It was when she rushed into the party and cried, "It's Binky! Binky is gone!"

The first time she said it, Binky ran to Annabel and shoved her onto the couch.

"Oof!" Annabel grunted.

Woof! Binky barked. He put his huge paw on her lap. He searched her face with big, worried eyes.

"Good job, Annabel!" Harvey Tuttle said. "You even had Binky worried."

Annabel tried to catch her breath. "I'd better try to be less realistic next time," she said.

They went through the play twice.

"Great work, gang!" Barbara said, after the second run-through. "Annabel, you're doing very well."

Annabel beamed. After all, when Barbara gave her the part, she didn't know that Annabel was a good actress. She only knew that Annabel didn't faint at the sight of giant dogs.

"Friday night we'll rehearse at Fairfax House," Barbara said.

Fairfax House was an old mansion just outside of town. The Friends of the Arts had rented it for the fund-raising play.

"We'll perform in the ballroom," Barbara said. "We won't have an actual stage."

Annabel was sitting on the floor. Sitting next to her, Binky's head was higher than hers. A lot higher.

"How will we keep Binky from running around and kissing the whole audience?" Annabel asked.

"He won't be able to get to them," Barbara said. "He'll be on a leash."

Annabel looked up at Binky's neck. It was so big and furry she wondered how Barbara had ever found a collar to fit it.

"And I'm going to be holding the leash?" Annabel asked.

"That's right." Barbara gave her a big, happy smile. "So I'm delighted that you and Binky have become such good friends."

Binky bent down and licked Annabel's hair.

"Uh, yes." Annabel winced as his cold, wet nose nudged her eyebrow. "I'm delighted, too."

Scene 5

Annabel at the Ballroom

"Wow!" Annabel stared. The ballroom at Fairfax House was the biggest room she had ever seen.

The ceiling was blue and gold with angels and clouds painted on it. The floor was made of dark, gleaming wood squares.

"This must have been beautiful when it was new," Betsy Cohen said.

Annabel thought it was still beautiful.

In the center of the room, a large white statue of a dolphin stood on its tail. Red velvet seats formed a circle around the dolphin.

"That's a fountain," Barbara said. "Wait till you see it with the water turned on."

Dinner tables and chairs were grouped on both sides of the dolphin fountain, in rows that went halfway to the back of the room.

Binky trotted around, sniffing everywhere.

He crawled under tables. He sniffed at the velvet benches. He made a big circle around the room. Then he came back to sit at Annabel's side.

Barbara pointed to the area in front of the dolphin. "This will be our stage," she said. "And on both sides of the fountain."

She showed the cast where she would hide the envelopes that held the clues to the kidnapper. The audience would have to find all the clue envelopes to solve the mystery. The actors would have to be careful not to move them.

To the left of the stage area, an arched opening led to a narrow hallway. At the end of the hall there was a small room.

"This is our cast room," Barbara said. She explained to Annabel that the actors would stay in the cast room in between scenes.

The first rehearsal took a long time. Barbara had to show the actors where to enter and exit, and where to stand and move during the play.

Binky was shut in the cast room, with the door closed. Annabel could hear him howling and whining all the way in the ballroom.

"He's making a lot of noise for a kidnapped dog," Manning Marlowe said.

"He'll be fine when we're doing the play," Barbara said. "Annabel will be with him most of the time."

Annabel hoped that Barbara had an extra costume for her. Or at least a blow-dryer. After half an hour with Binky, she would be extremely soggy.

The second rehearsal went much faster than the first. Barbara smiled and clapped when it was over.

"I can hardly believe this is only our fourth run-through!"

Annabel was proud of herself. She had remembered all her lines. That wasn't hard. But she had really *felt* her role as Polly Morfus.

She kept thinking about her deep, dark secret. She remembered how worried she was about her father. Was the butler the Crestview jewel thief? Was he Binky's kidnapper?

She thought of how she would go to college, and invent something and become rich. She imagined how she would take care of her father so he wouldn't have to be a butler anymore. Or a jewel thief.

And during rehearsals, Binky wouldn't leave her side. When she cried, "It's Binky! Binky is gone!" she really felt as if she had lost her best friend.

As everyone climbed into Barbara's van to go home after rehearsal, Barbara said, "Oh! Annabel, I almost forgot."

She took a large canvas bag from the back of the van. "Your costume," she said.

She pulled something pink and fuzzy from the bag.

"What is that?" Annabel asked.

"Bunny pajamas."

Barbara grinned as she held them up against Annabel. "Aren't they adorable?"

Annabel looked down at the costume. She looked up at Barbara. "It has feet!" she cried. "And ears!"

"I think it will fit perfectly," Barbara went on, as if she hadn't heard Annabel.

"But I'm the butler's daughter!" Annabel said. "I have a deep, dark secret! I shouldn't be dressed like a bunny."

"That's the whole idea," Barbara said. "We want the audience to wonder if you're as young and innocent as you look."

"But—"

Barbara tucked the pajamas under Annabel's arm. "Wear them for dress rehearsal next Friday night," she said. "I can't *wait* to see you in them."

Scene 6

The Footprints of a Fuzzy Bunny

"COSTUME EMERGENCY!" Annabel screamed into the phone. "Maggie, HELP!"

She tossed the bunny pajamas onto her bed. She stared at them. The long, pink ears. The clumpy, fuzzy feet.

She was embarrassed just looking at the costume. How could she possibly act in it?

The doorbell rang. Six times. Annabel ran to the front door and yanked it open.

"What's the emergency?" Maggie was already in her own pajamas. "And do you know what time it is?"

"Yes," said Annabel. She led Maggie into her room. "But this is a real emergency."

She pointed to her bed. Maggie walked over to the bed and picked up Annabel's costume. "You're playing a rabbit?" she asked. "I thought you were supposed to be the butler's daughter."

37

"I *am* the butler's daughter," Annabel said. "These are my pajamas."

Maggie picked up the costume. She ran her hand over the ears. She frowned. "Polyester."

"I don't care what they're made of!" Annabel wailed. "I don't want to act in my first real play wearing bunny pajamas!"

Maggie turned the costume around in her hands. "I could cut off the feet," she began, "and the hood with the ears—"

"You can't cut anything," Annabel said. "It's not mine."

"Then how am I supposed to fix it?" Maggie asked.

"I don't know! You're my costume designer!"

"I'm a designer," Maggie said, "not a magician. I can't pull rabbits out of hats."

"Very funny." Annabel threw herself onto the bed and held her arm over her eyes. "How would you feel doing a whole play in this costume?"

"Extremely dumb," Maggie said. She bit her lip. She frowned. She turned the bunny pajamas over and over in her hands.

"I'll be right back," she said.

"Do you have an idea?" Annabel asked hopefully.

But Maggie had already dashed out of her room. The front door opened and slammed shut.

A few minutes later, Maggie was back.

"I'm a genius," she announced. "Put the costume on."

Annabel pulled the bunny pajamas on

over her clothes. Maggie opened the first two snaps on the front. She tucked the hood and the ears inside the back of the pajamas.

She wrapped a bright, flowery Japanese kimono around Annabel.

She pushed Annabel in front of the mirror on her closet door. "See?" Maggie said. "Now you have chic lounging pajamas."

Annabel looked in the mirror. The kimono had pink and orange and yellow flowers on a black background. But it was long. Very long. Half of it puddled on the floor.

"Don't you think it's a little big?" Annabel asked.

"No problem," said Maggie. "My mother told me I could take up the hem. As long as I don't cut anything."

She whipped a tape measure out of the pocket of her bathrobe. "Stand still," she ordered.

Annabel stood still as Maggie measured and pinned the hem of the kimono.

"What can we do about these?" Annabel pointed to her fuzzy pink feet.

"I could cut them off," Maggie said. "And make the legs into capri pants. That would be very chic."

"You can't cut them off," Annabel said. "It's Barbara's costume. Besides, I don't think she wants me to look chic."

"Then there's nothing to worry about." Maggie stuck the last three pins into the bottom of the kimono. "Fuzzy pink feet are never chic."

A Fatal Dryer Accident

On the night of the dress rehearsal, Annabel's father drove her to Fairfax House.

"I hope we don't get into an accident," Annabel said. She was wearing the bunny pajamas and the kimono under her jacket.

"I hope not, too," her father said.

"I wouldn't want anyone at the hospital to see me in these stupid pajamas," Annabel grumbled.

Barbara and the rest of the cast were just getting out of Barbara's van when Annabel arrived.

"I'll drive her home when we're done," Barbara told her father. "We might be late, though, so don't worry."

In the ballroom, everyone took off their coats. Nervously, Annabel pulled off her jacket and put it on the back of a chair.

"Annabel, where is your costume?" Barbara asked sharply.

"I'm wearing it," Annabel said. "I just put a robe over it."

"A robe isn't part of your costume," Barbara said.

"But I was thinking about it," Annabel began, "and I wouldn't want all those strangers to see me in pajamas. Even if I am only the butler's daughter."

"The butler's daughter wouldn't be wearing a silk kimono, either," Barbara said.

Annabel sighed deeply. She untied the sash of the kimono, slipped it off, and draped it over her jacket.

"There, that's the way I pictured you," Barbara said. "You look just darling."

Annabel scowled. Betsy Cohen and Janice Taylor exchanged glances. Annabel knew they were embarrassed for her.

Much as Annabel hated her costume, Binky loved it. He spent a good part of the rehearsal sniffing it, licking it, and rubbing

his nose against the pink fur.

"What did you do to that bunny suit?" Stan Taylor asked. "Smear liver on it?"

"No," Annabel said. "I did not smear liver on it."

When dress rehearsal ended, Annabel couldn't wait to get out of her costume. The fur was sticky and damp, and the costume looked even worse than it had when she had first put it on.

"I hope Binky isn't going to chew on me during the play," she said to Barbara. "Maybe I should wear something he doesn't like so much."

"Oh, no!" Barbara said. "You look perfect just the way you are."

Annabel was holding the bunny pajamas by two fingers when she walked into her house. They had dried off a little, but now they smelled like drooly dog.

"Annabel, is that you?" her father called from upstairs.

She dropped the pajamas in the kitchen sink and went up to her parents' bedroom.

"How did rehearsal go?" he asked. Annabel's mother was asleep, with her pillow over one ear.

The TV was on, very softly.

"Good," Annabel said. "Except for Binky trying to eat my costume. I'm going to go wash it out."

"Do you need any help?" her father asked.

"No thanks," said Annabel. "What are you watching?"

"*Kickin' Cajun Cookin',*" her father said. "But I don't know how anyone can eat Five Alarm Jalapeno Chicken."

"Binky could," Annabel said.

She went downstairs to the kitchen. She filled the sink with warm water and swished the bunny pajamas around in it. She squirted dishwashing liquid over them. She squeezed and rubbed and rinsed the costume three times.

Then she went to the basement and put the bunny pajamas into the dryer.

She looked at the settings on the dryer: DELICATE, PERMANENT PRESS, COTTON.

Annabel was sure the costume wasn't delicate. Maggie had said it was polyester, so it couldn't be cotton.

She decided on "Permanent Press" and set the timer for sixty minutes.

She went upstairs and flopped backward onto her bed. She was so tired. School, and dress rehearsal, and Binky, and laundry—it had been a long day.

She should get undressed and wash and go to sleep. The dryer would stop automatically. She didn't have to wait up for it to finish drying her costume.

"That's what I'll do," Annabel said to herself. "I'll get undressed and . . ." Before she could finish the thought, she was asleep.

The next thing she heard was someone far away, yelling.

Annabel sat up in bed. The yelling was coming from the basement. A strange, burnt smell was also coming from the basement.

She ran downstairs.

"What's wrong?" she cried. "What is that smell?"

Her father was hopping around, stamping his feet on something.

"Your costume caught fire," her father said.

He picked up the thing he had been stamping on. It was black at the ears, and the feet had melted.

"I thought you fixed the dryer!" Annabel said.

Annabel's mother put her arms around

Annabel. "Honey, you can't put plastic in a dryer."

"But I didn't!" Annabel cried. "I just put the stupid bunny pajamas in it!"

"The feet," her mother said. "The bottoms of the feet, and the inside of the ears. They're plastic—I mean, *were* plastic."

Annabel took the bunny pajamas from her father. She held them up. They were a charred, ragged mess.

"They're ruined!" Annabel said.

Her mother nodded. "I'm afraid they are."

"Then . . . I can't wear them," Annabel said slowly.

"I don't think so," her mother said.

Annabel thought about this for a moment.

"Oh," she said. "What a pity."

Hound of the Barkervilles

"Oh, it's so beautiful!"

It was opening night, and Annabel felt as if she were in another world.

The dinner tables at Fairfax House were covered with snowy white tablecloths. Flowers and candles were everywhere. Silvery water sprayed from the dolphin fountain's mouth.

Binky trotted to the fountain and stuck his head under the spray. He *woofed* cheerfully. He trotted back to Annabel and shook himself off.

"One way or another," she said, "you

manage to be a very wet dog."

"I'll put out the clue envelopes," Barbara said, "and meet you in the cast room."

Barbara was already in her costume. She was playing Mrs. Van Barkerville, the hostess of the party. She wore a long dress with silver sequins and fringes.

Annabel was carrying what was left of the bunny pajamas in a plastic Record World shopping bag. The kimono was in there, too, along with a pair of yellow-and-black bumblebee slippers that her grandmother had given her.

Annabel changed in the small bathroom next to the cast room. She put on what was left of the bunny pajamas. She tucked the ruined ears and hood into the back, behind her neck.

She put the kimono on over the pajamas, and tied the sash. She stepped into the slippers. They were yellow, with chubby black-and-yellow striped bees on top of the toes.

They were too big. But one had to fit over the bunny foot that hadn't burned.

"What happened to your costume?" Betsy Cohen asked, as Annabel walked back into the cast room.

"My father tried to fix the dryer," Annabel said. "There was a terrible accident."

Binky paced nervously around the room.

"Opening night jitters," Stan said.

Annabel knew how he felt.

She'd been in plenty of school plays. But this was her first play where the audience wasn't all parents.

Manning Marlowe opened the door of the cast room a crack, to hear what was happening in the ballroom.

Cheerful voices and lively music drifted into the room.

"Showtime!" Barbara flung the door open.

"Owwf!" Man- ning   Marlowe

staggered out from behind the door, holding his nose.

"Oh, Manning, I'm sorry!" Barbara said.

Binky made a break for the open door. Annabel grabbed his collar just in time. "Not yet, Binky."

"Okay, everyone," Barbara said. "Break a leg."

Annabel knew that "break a leg" meant "good luck."

Harvey Tuttle smoothed his white gloves. He picked up a feather duster. Annabel watched him get into character as a butler.

He stooped his shoulders a little. He moved slowly toward the door. He held his head high. Before he even left the room, you could tell he was old, but proud.

That is very good acting, Annabel told herself.

"Get ready, Polly," Barbara said. "You're on in one minute."

"I'm ready." Annabel handed Binky's leash to Janice.

"Wait!" Barbara turned Annabel around

and took a long look at her. "What happened to your costume?"

"I'll explain later." Before Barbara could say another word, Annabel darted out the door.

She stopped in the hallway, right at the entrance to the ballroom. She took a deep breath.

"I am Polly," she recited to herself. "I have a deep, dark secret."

She took another breath. "I am poor but honest. I am only the butler's daughter. But some-day . . ."

She walked into the ballroom. She crossed the floor, and stopped next to Harvey. "Are there going to be a lot of people at the party tonight, Father?" she asked.

The audience began to quiet down. Chairs

scraped on the floor as people took their seats.

"A lot of rich people," Harvey said. "Why, the jewels in this house tonight will be worth a king's ransom."

"I hope the Crestview jewel thief doesn't know about the party," Annabel said. She gave Harvey a meaningful look.

Barbara, playing Mrs. Van Barkerville, rushed into the ballroom.

"Oh, Morfus!" she said to Harvey. "What shall we do? Harley Golightly, the interna-

tional sportsman and playboy, is coming to the party after all."

"We might seat him next to Senorita Lolita Lopez," Harvey said. "They are both members of the jet set. They should get along nicely."

"How clever, Morfus," Barbara said. "Whatever would I do without you?"

Harvey bowed his head slightly. "I hope you will never have to, Madam."

He turned to Annabel. "Polly," he said, "it's time for Binky's evening walk. Take him to Axel Greece, the chauffeur."

"All right, Father." Annabel started toward the archway exit. "I hope the party is—" she began.

A shrill voice interrupted her line.

"That's not the butler's daughter!" it yelled. "That's Annabel!"

Scene 9

An Enemy in the Audience

Lowell Boxer! Annabel's lifelong enemy! What was he doing here? The play was supposed to be for adults only.

"Be quiet!" someone whispered loudly.
"Shh!" someone else said.
Annabel searched the audience for Lowell. She spotted him sitting at table number six.

His mother was whispering something in his ear.

The other people at his table looked annoyed.

"I'll go get Binky," Annabel said quickly, and hurried off stage. She didn't know what else to do, except that she had to ignore Lowell.

Janice, Stan, and Betsy were in the hall, waiting for their cues.

"What was that all about?" Stan asked.

"That was Lowell Boxer," Annabel said, very angry. "My worst enemy. He will try to ruin the play."

"Why would he do that?" Betsy asked.

Annabel scowled. "He is not a Friend of the Arts."

Now Annabel had to wait in the cast room until it was time to walk Binky across the ballroom floor.

Binky was so good, she could hardly believe it. He didn't bark or whine or try to knock the door down. He just lay quietly at Annabel's feet. Every once in a while he poked his nose into the bumblebee on top of one of her slippers and sneezed.

Annabel tried not to think about Lowell. *I will just ignore him,* she told herself, *No matter what he does.*

She waited in the cast room, reminding herself not to think about Lowell. Then she picked up Binky's leash and led him into the hallway. She heard Harvey speak her cue.

"Would you care for a cocktail, Lady Ashley?"

"Here we go," Annabel whispered to Binky. "Be good. Don't eat any of the audience."

She walked into the ballroom. He followed her as far as Betsy Cohen, who was Lady Ashley. Then he stopped. He looked around at all the people. His rear end began to wiggle. His tongue hung out of his mouth. He drooled.

Annabel felt him tugging at the leash.

He does want to eat the audience! she thought. *I knew it!*

For a moment she didn't know what to do. Then she said, "Come, Binky!" and pulled hard on the leash. "Maybe you can meet the guests later."

The line wasn't in the script. But she had to say something. She couldn't just stand there staring at the audience.

She was surprised when Binky obeyed. He turned away from the audience and started to follow Annabel across the floor.

"Yo, Annabel!" Lowell yelled. "What's with the stupid shoes?"

Annabel froze.

WOOF!

Binky leaped forward. Annabel struggled to hold onto the leash. But Binky pulled so hard, he dragged her along behind him. She

slid across the smooth, shiny floor, her slippers gliding like skis.

"Binky, no!" she cried.

"No, Binky!" Harvey's voice was like thunder.

Binky stopped short next to the dolphin fountain. He stopped so suddenly that Annabel nearly tumbled forward over him.

Harvey took the leash and wrapped it twice around Annabel's wrist.

"He certainly is eager for his walk tonight, isn't he, Polly?"

"Yes, Father." Annabel gave Harvey a weak grin.

"Get along then." Harvey patted her on the shoulder.

She held onto the leash so tightly that her wrist hurt. But Binky followed her obediently out the exit.

In the cast room, she flopped into a chair and groaned.

"Didn't I tell you?" she said to Binky. "Didn't I tell you not to try and eat the audience?"

Binky drooled cheerfully. He thumped his tail on the floor.

"Well, okay," Annabel said. "It was mostly Lowell's fault for yelling. But you shouldn't have tried to run away."

Binky cocked his head to one side and

watched her talk. His eyes were big and curious.

Annabel sighed. She rubbed his head. "Look, Binky, one of you has to act mature. And you know it's not going to be Lowell."

She took some deep, cleansing breaths. She had only two more lines to say. She had to rush into the party and shout that Binky was gone.

"I don't care what Lowell does," she repeated. "I don't care what he says. I will ignore him."

She went out into the hall, closing Binky in the cast room. She walked to the archway and waited for her cue.

"Dinner is served," Harvey announced.

Annabel took another deep breath. *Focus!* She told herself. *I feel panic! Fear! Upsetness!*

She ran into the ballroom. Her slippers made shuffle-*thwack* sounds on the wood floor.

"Oh, oh!" she cried. "It's Binky! Binky is gone!"

Get a Clue

"We're a hit, kids!" Barbara said.

The actors were in the cast room, resting before they had to mix in with the guests. Janice had kicked off her very high-heeled shoes and was rubbing her feet.

"Annabel, you were great!" Barbara said. "Too bad about Lowell."

"But what was he doing here?" Annabel said. "The play was supposed to be adults only."

"Carol Boxer couldn't find a baby-sitter," Barbara explained. "How could I tell her not to come?"

"Can she *ever* find a baby-sitter?" Manning Marlowe asked.

"Take five more minutes," Barbara said. "Then it's question time."

This was the part of the performance that

Annabel had worried about most. She'd never had to think up her own lines before. But on the plus side, now she would be able to say anything she pleased to Lowell.

She began to think of some things she wanted to say to Lowell.

Janice put her shoes back on. Manning Marlowe smoothed down his mustache.

"Now, Annabel," Barbara said, "Tell me. Why aren't you wearing the costume I gave you?"

"I am," Annabel said. She untied the sash of the kimono.

Barbara gasped when she saw the charred, ragged bunny suit. "What happened to it?"

Annabel closed the kimono and tied the sash.

"My father is not very good at fixing dryers," she said.

The actors moved into the ballroom, and Annabel looked around for Lowell. She didn't see him anywhere. Maybe Mrs. Boxer had taken him home and put him to bed without dinner.

A buffet table loaded with food was set up at the back of the ballroom. Waiters and waitresses walked among the guests, offering canapés.

Annabel was starving. She headed for the buffet. A man and a woman stopped her as she was about to help herself to some grapes.

"Little girl," the man said, "aren't you the butler's daughter?"

"Yes, sir."

"I'll give you five dollars if you tell us who kidnapped the dog."

"What?" Annabel was so shocked, she forgot about acting. The man was trying to cheat!

She looked at him sternly. "I don't know, sir," she said. "It's a mystery."

"Come on, Harold," the woman said. She plucked at his sleeve. "She's no help."

They walked away, and Annabel reached across the buffet table for a bunch of grapes.

"You look like a dork."

She dropped the grapes. She whirled around. Lowell Boxer was standing right behind her. His mouth was full. He was chewing noisily.

Annabel glared at him. "And you have disgusting manners."

Lowell grabbed a fistful of cheese cubes from the table. He reached into his pocket and pulled out a miniature frankfurter on a toothpick. He shoved it into his mouth.

"I don't care," he said, chewing. "At least I don't look dorky."

"You look porky," Annabel said. "As in, pig."

She walked away, trying to be dignified. Mrs. Boxer was standing near table six. *If I stay near her,* Annabel thought, *Lowell won't dare do anything bad.*

"Annabel, you were wonderful!" Mrs. Boxer said.

"Thank you, ma'am," Annabel said. "But my name is Polly."

"Of course." Lowell's mother winked. "Well, you were wonderful, Polly."

"I do my best, ma'am."

Lowell marched to table six carrying two heaping plates of food.

"Why, thank you for bringing me a plate, dear." Mrs. Boxer smiled.

Lowell looked at her blankly. "I didn't," he said.

With Lowell busy stuffing his mouth with food, Annabel went back to mixing with the crowd. Only a few people asked her any questions. Barbara must have been right. Annabel's costume made her look young and innocent. Even with the kimono.

The questions were easy to answer, too. Annabel never forgot that she was Polly, the butler's daughter. Young and innocent, but with a mysterious secret.

Until a man in a dark suit taped her on the shoulder.

"Little girl," he said sharply. "When was the last time you saw the dog alive?"

Uh-oh. Annabel tried to think. She didn't know what time she had brought Binky to Axel. How could Barbara have forgotten to tell her something so important?

Think fast!

"Saw him *alive?*" she cried. "Oh, sir, do you think Binky is dead?" She burst into loud sobs. "If anything's happened to Binky, I'll never forgive myself!"

The man stared at her as she collapsed into a chair and buried her face in her hands.

She sniffled loudly. Her shoulders shook.

She created a very good diversion.

Right in the middle of her diversion, she heard a yell from the front of the ballroom.

She looked up.

Binky was galloping toward her, with Lowell racing after him.

"I found him!" Lowell shouted. "I found Binky! Can we have dessert now?"

Scene 11

Whodunnit

Annabel wanted to scream. How could Lowell be so mean? Why did he want to ruin the play? Even if he was her lifelong enemy, why spoil the play for everyone else?

She jumped from her chair and ran to Lowell. She yanked Binky's leash out of his hand.

"This isn't Binky!"

Everyone in the ballroom stopped talking. They stopped eating. All eyes were on Annabel.

What do I do now? She asked herself. She shut her eyes and tried to think. *Say something! Anything!*

"This is *not* Binky!" She said again. She gulped. "This is . . . this is . . . Binky's evil twin!"

"What?" Lowell gawked at her.

"Come on, Stinky." Annabel pulled at Binky's leash, and led him toward the exit.

"He is too Binky!" Lowell yelled.

"No, he is not," Annabel said firmly. "He is Stinky. And you're lucky he didn't rip your throat out. He hates nasty little boys."

She ran offstage, Binky trotting after her. In the cast room, she leaned against a wall, shaking with anger.

Barbara and Manning rushed into the room.

"Annabel, you're a genius!" Barbara said.

"He makes me so mad!" Annabel squeezed

her eyes shut and clenched her fists. Binky nosed her elbow and whimpered.

"It wasn't your fault this time," she said to Binky. She rubbed her cheek against the top of his head. "Lowell is a very bad influence."

"But you were excellent," Manning said. "A real trooper."

"I was?" Annabel smiled gratefully. "Thank you." She rubbed Binky's ear. "You're a real trooper too," she said to him. "Mostly."

While the audience ate dessert and worked on solving the mystery, the actors had sandwiches in the cast room. Annabel slipped half of her sandwich under the table to Binky.

Manning went to the ballroom to collect the solutions. Each table formed a team of detectives, who had worked on the mystery together.

Manning brought back a batch of answer sheets.

Barbara read through them quickly. She held up one piece of paper. "We have a winner," she said.

She took a small gold and white trophy from her canvas bag. "Let's go," she said.

Back in the ballroom, Barbara announced, "It's time to solve the mystery!"

The audience stopped eating dessert. They looked at the actors and began to whisper excitedly.

"Who kidnapped Binky? Was it Axel Greece, the chauffeur?"

Stan stepped forward and scowled at the audience.

"Was it Senorita Lolita Lopez?"

Janice twirled around and stretched her black veil across her lips.

"Abel Morfus?" Barbara went on. "The butler with a dark past? Polly Morfus, his young daughter?"

Annabel and Harvey stepped forward. Annabel looked around at the audience mysteriously.

"I'll bet it was her!" a shrill voice called.

Annabel stepped back into line with the other actors. "When this is over," she whis-

pered to Binky, "you can eat him."

"And the winning team . . ." Barbara stopped for a dramatic pause. ". . . correctly guessed that the dognapper was Harley Golightly, the international sportsman and playboy. He dognapped Binky, the prize-winning show dog, to sell him to CurlyQ Kennels for fifty thousand dollars."

Barbara read from the piece of paper she held. "And the winning team is . . . table number six!"

"Woo hoo!" Lowell Boxer leaped out of his chair, knocking it over. He dashed between tables and around the dolphin fountain.

He grabbed the trophy from Barbara, and lifted it over his head.

"We're number one!" he shouted.

He ran back to table six, waving the statue. "We won, we won!"

"This is not the ending I had hoped for," Annabel said.

Scene
12

A Perfect Ending

The actors joined hands and bowed. Annabel stood between Barbara and Harvey and bowed low. The audience clapped and cheered. Some of them even whistled and stamped their feet.

Binky *woofed* and started to shuffle around Annabel's legs.

"Listen," Annabel whispered to him. "We were good!" She felt the applause wrap around her like a warm hug.

There's nothing like performing in front of a live audience, she thought. *This has to be the best feeling in the world.*

"Aren't we EVER going to get out of here?" Lowell's shout was loud enough to be heard over the applause.

Harvey rolled his eyes.

Somehow Binky's leash slipped right through Annabel's fingers. When the leash dropped to the floor, Binky realized he was free.

He ran straight for table number six.

When Lowell saw Binky charging at him, he scrambled onto the table. Coffee cups went flying. Water goblets crashed to the floor. A cream pitcher overturned and spilled into a woman's lap.

Woof! Binky stood on his hind legs. His two front paws landed on two leftover plates of strawberry shortcake.

He licked his paw curiously. Then he started tugging at Lowell's pants.

"Get him away! Get him *away!*" Lowell tried to crawl across the table to escape from Binky. But Binky held onto his pants. Lowell turned over and tried to sit up. Binky started licking whipped cream and strawberries off his face.

"Don't be frightened, Lowell!" Barbara shouted, as she raced to table six.

"Get him off!" Lowell screamed. "He's trying to eat me!"

"He won't hurt you." Barbara grabbed Binky's collar.

Binky backed up, panting. He *woofed* happily.

Lowell's face was red. His hair stood up in sticky spikes. His shirt was a mess of strawberries and whipped cream and coffee.

The other guests at table six were trying to wipe water and cake off their clothes. They glared at Lowell and Binky.

"I'm so sorry," Barbara apologized. "I don't know what got into him."

She dragged Binky to the front of the ball-room.

"Naughty Binky," she scolded. "What kind of way is that to end our play?"

"The perfect way." Annabel whispered, and kissed Binky right on his big, furry head.